# TEMPTED

## ELIZABETH KELLY

EK PUBLISHING INC.

TEMPTED

**Losing control has never felt so good.**

Lucy Reid has always prided herself on her self-control, and her ability to keep her emotions and desires in check.

The arrival of her new boss, Jason Young, has her co-workers competing to see who can bed him first. Lucy refuses to admit her own attraction to him, and his rude behavior towards her only strengthens her resolve to ignore her growing attraction.

When a power outage traps her in the elevator with her sexy new boss, she soon realizes his coldness hides his own dark desire for her. Jason Young is determined to show her just how good it can feel to lose control, and Lucy is aching to give in to the sweet temptation.

# CHAPTER 1

"No, no, no," Lucy muttered under her breath. She thought briefly of pushing the 'close doors' button before holding the door instead.

He slipped through the elevator doors and nodded his thanks. As the doors closed and the elevator hummed its way down to the parking garage, he glanced at her. "You're working late this evening, Ms. Reid."

She smiled stiffly at him. He was the reason she was working late when she should have been out celebrating Amanda's birthday with the rest of her friends. She sighed and brushed at a speck of lint on her skirt.

It wasn't that she hated her new boss. She just really, really disliked him. Jason Young was by far the most arrogant, egotistical jackass she'd ever had to work for. It didn't matter that in the last six months he had taken their small, unassuming website and turned it into one of the most-viewed websites of the year. Nor did it matter that he had secured so many new advertisers that everyone in the office had received a bonus and ten percent raise. She knew he was good at what he did - it's why he was hired in the first place. The problem was that she was a damn fine copy editor and she worked her ass off for the company, but for some mysterious reason Jason Young loathed her.

Today was particularly brutal. She had stayed positive only by reminding herself that it was Friday, and she could forget the day with a few, well-timed tequila shots at Amanda's birthday party. Of course, thanks to Mr. Young, that plan was shot after lunch.

She sighed again and glanced at her cell phone. It was only eight thirty. She could go home, change into something slinky and sexy and still meet the gang at the pub. She realized that her boss was standing a little closer and staring silently at her.

She shot him a dirty look before returning her gaze to her cell phone. She was off the clock. There was no need to be friendly or polite with him.

"Ms. Reid, do you have a problem with me?" he asked suddenly.

"Why would you think that?" she asked.

"Because you -"

The elevator came to a sudden, grinding halt. The lights went out, plunging them into darkness, and she was thrown against him. Her cell phone flew out of her hand and hit the elevator wall with a crunching noise that made her wince.

She shrank against him, her heart thudding in her chest. With a low buzz, the emergency lights came on and bathed the elevator in a dim red light. She was still pressed against him with panicked intimacy. He was holding her with his large hands clamped around her full hips, and she flushed and shoved at his hard chest.

"Let go of me."

"Just wait a minute, I think -"

She gasped as the elevator made another groaning lurch

and dropped a few more feet. Her stomach dropped with it, and her fear made her clutch to his broad shoulders.

"What the hell?" she said.

He frowned. "The elevator seems to be broken."

She pushed again at his chest. "Let me go, please."

His gaze dropped to her mouth and lingered there. His stare, combined with the warmth of his hands on her hips, was making her skin tingle. She licked her lips nervously. His gaze darkened and his nostrils flared, and she stared mesmerized at the dark stubble that covered his lower face. She was struck by the urge to kiss the dark shadow, to lick it with her tongue and feel it prickle against her lips. She was actually leaning forward when he gently pushed her away.

She turned away, utterly mortified by her behavior, and wondered briefly if she could pry the doors open and climb down the elevator shaft to get away from him. Instead, she walked gingerly across the elevator to rescue her cell phone. He opened the control panel door and picked up the black telephone receiver that was attached to it. He held the receiver to his ear, waiting patiently.

Lucy stared at her cell phone and muttered a curse. The screen was shattered but she pushed a few buttons, knowing it was pointless but trying anyway.

"Shit," she muttered.

He scowled at her and made a shushing gesture with his hand. "Yes, hello? This is Jason Young from the twenty-seventh floor. It seems our elevator has broken down."

She shoved her phone into her purse and tried not to think about the fact that there was no way out. Already her chest was tightening and the air in the elevator seemed too warm. She wasn't exactly claustrophobic, but it was useless to deny that tight spaces made her uncomfortable.

She fanned herself with the top of her blouse before

3

unbuttoning her suit jacket and removing it. She placed it neatly on the floor of the elevator as he hung up the phone.

"Are they sending someone to fix it?" she asked.

He shrugged out of his own suit jacket, and she ignored the way his white dress shirt clung to his powerful shoulders and accentuated his wide chest.

"Apparently the power is out to the entire block - some kind of power surge. Until they can get the power back on, we're stuck in here."

"Double shit." She looked up at the ceiling panels. "Can't they send in, I don't know, firemen or someone to open up the ceiling and let us out that way?"

He gave her a wry look. "I doubt that two people stuck in an elevator is a top priority for them right now, Ms. Reid."

She flushed at his condescending tone and fanned herself with her shirt again. Sweat was starting to trickle between her breasts and she unbuttoned the top two buttons and stuck her head down her top, blowing lightly to try and cool herself.

---

JASON WATCHED AS LUCY UNBUTTONED THE TOP TWO buttons of her shirt. He nearly groaned out loud when it revealed her smooth, pale skin and a hint of cleavage. He'd had numerous fantasies about seeing her round, full breasts. But in the six months since he joined the firm, she had never worn anything that didn't button nearly to her throat. She favoured tailored business suits that hid her breasts and downplayed the generous curve of her ass.

He had realized how temptingly full and ripe her breasts were about a month after he started. It was another late night and he was on his way home when he had glanced casually into her office as he walked by. She was standing in front of

4

the window, her jacket and shoes lying forgotten on the floor and her hands in the small of her back. She was stretching, and he had gotten an immediate and embarrassing erection at the sight of her large breasts straining enticingly at the fabric of her shirt.

He had stared at her for a few moments, memorizing every line of her curvy body before hurrying down the hallway with his dick throbbing and his pulse pounding. Since that night, he could barely be around her without wondering what it would be like to pull her jacket off, slip his hands under her silk top, and cup those magnificent breasts.

As she blew down her shirt again, he let his eyes drift over her face. She was an attractive woman. There was something about her cheekbones and the curve of her full lips that just about made his heart stop. Her dark hair was pulled into its usual twist, but by this late in the evening a few strands had escaped and were curling around her neck. He wondered how long her hair was. He wondered if it was as silky as it looked, and wondered how it would feel draped across his thighs as she used that generous mouth to —

He groaned to himself and dragged his gaze away from her, willing his erection to go down. He had never acted inappropriately with an employee before, and he was annoyed by his lack of self-control around her. She wasn't just beautiful, he thought. She had proved to be smart and efficient at her job and her direct supervisor, Jerry Hanson, couldn't say enough good things about her. Still, he'd fought his growing attraction to her by being cold and rude, and she'd responded with her own chilliness.

Lucy cleared her throat and stared at him, her dark eyes wide with anxiety. "How long do you think it will be?"

He shrugged and loosened his tie, pulling it over his head

and dropping it to the floor next to his suit jacket before unbuttoning two buttons of his own shirt. "I don't know."

---

LUCY'S EYES DROPPED TO JASON'S CHEST. SHE COULD SEE A hint of dark, curly hair, and she moistened her suddenly dry lips with her tongue. Sweat beaded up on her brow, and she wiped her palms against her skirt.

Why did he have to be so goddamn attractive? It would be much easier to ignore him if he wasn't the typical tall, dark and handsome type that regularly invaded her dreams. Not that there was any point to dreaming about him. Guys like Jason Young didn't fall for girls like her.

He would favour the tall, thin, and blonde model types with their flawless tanned skin and perfect hair. At 5'9" she fit the bill for being tall, but her thick, dark hair was impossible to tame, her skin pale and prone to blotchiness when she was nervous, and her chunky body would never be mistaken for a model's.

She could and did attract plenty of male attention. She dressed for her body shape and she was proud of her curves. Her thighs might touch, and her stomach might not be perfectly flat, but she knew how to work with her assets - especially her breasts. No one here would know it - at the office she preferred to wear clothing that downplayed her chest - but outside of work she wore tight shirts with low neck lines that showcased her firm cleavage.

She had an active dating life. Or did, she amended. Since Jason was hired six months ago, her sex life had died out dramatically. It was hard to get laid when you were spending most of your free time at the office. It was yet another reason to dislike him.

She leaned against the elevator wall. She seemed to be the only woman in the office who didn't like him. He could be, and was often, charming to the other women. And when he chose to use it, his smile weakened the knees of every female employee in the building. Even Carol, the fifty-seven-year-old receptionist who had a grudge toward almost every man she came across, giggled like a schoolgirl when he turned on the charm.

She snorted to herself. About two months ago, a bet was started among the ladies she worked with. The goal, of course, was to see who could bed their new boss first. They had even pooled their money to buy a prize - a weekend of pampering at 'Heaven's Gate Spa'.

They hadn't bothered to invite her into the betting pool. His rude behavior toward her, the extra pounds she carried, and her absolute refusal to wear anything that was even remotely suggestive had them convinced she wouldn't have a chance with their handsome new boss.

She was both appalled and a little amused at their behavior. Despite her dislike for him, her brain was quick to inform her that it was inclined to believe the prize was pointless. That, in fact, the prize itself would be getting to bed Jason Young. To find out what it was like to have him between her legs, and to feel his hard cock sliding deep into her while she moaned and shuddered below him.

She closed her eyes as a shiver of desire went down her body. Would he be rough or gentle? Would he ask permission or just take what he wanted? She bit at her lip. It was a stupid question - he would take what he wanted. He was a man who liked to be in control. She knew that much from working with him for the past six months. He radiated a combination of confidence and arrogance that she refused to admit turned her on.

The men she slept with were always the same type. Shy, maybe even a little timid, they were drawn to her self-confidence like bees to honey and they were always willing to give up control in the bedroom.

She enjoyed it. She loved seeing the look on their faces when she peeled off her bra for the first time. She loved the way they moaned when she rode them, keeping her own need under a tight band of control as she brought them closer and closer. She couldn't even seem to give up that control when it came to her own orgasms. She controlled the pace, the need, and always came when *she* wanted to, not when they wanted her to.

*Jason wouldn't be like that.*

There was no reason for her to know that about him, but she knew it was the truth. He wouldn't let her take control, wouldn't allow her to decide when she came or how often. He would…

She realized with horror that her nipples had tightened in her bra until they were hard pebbles. She groaned inwardly. She hated losing control. Only one man had ever made her lose control - her first boyfriend. He had taken advantage of her willingness to do whatever it took to keep him, before finally dumping her in a spectacularly public fashion. She had vowed to never let a man control her emotions or thoughts again. Until the moment Jason Young joined their company, she had never wavered from that vow.

By the end of his first week, she was hopelessly attracted to him despite her dislike for him. It didn't matter how often she told herself that he was the exact opposite of what she wanted. It didn't even seem to matter how rude he was to her, just looking at him made her nipples hard and her pussy wet.

She ran a trembling hand over her forehead, wiping away the perspiration and trying to control her thoughts. What she was thinking about was incredibly inappropriate and besides, he hated her. Nothing would ever happen between them.

She fanned herself again and decided that it was not her inappropriate thoughts that were making the elevator feel so warm. Although her boss still looked crisp and unflappable, she could see a drop of sweat rolling slowly down his neck. She had a brief image of licking that trickle of moisture from his tanned skin and a slow throb started between her thighs.

She realized he was watching her watch him, his face a mixture of amusement and something else she couldn't read, and she blushed furiously. She could practically feel the blotchiness starting up on her chest and she stared down at the floor, hoping her still-hard nipples weren't visible through her blouse. She had to get a hold of herself. He might be handsome, and his deep voice might send shivers down her spine, but she was determined to curb her attraction to him. He was an asshole, plain and simple.

She folded her arms over her ample chest and glanced around the elevator. "It's really warm in here. Do you think there's enough, uh, oxygen?"

He smiled a little. "I never took you for the claustrophobic type, Ms. Reid."

"I'm not," she said. "I just don't like being stuck in small places."

"That, of course, being the very definition of a claustrophobic," he said.

"Whatever," she muttered testily. "Jesus, I hope it isn't much longer."

"Plans for the evening?" He raised one eyebrow at her.

"As a matter of fact, yes I do have plans - a birthday party for a good friend. Of course, it started over an hour ago. Unfortunately, I had to work late *again*."

"Be better at your job and you won't have to stay so late."

She gaped at him. "What did you say?"

He shrugged and leaned against the wall of the elevator. The late hour and the growing heat in the elevator had turned her neatly pressed top and skirt into a wrinkled mess, and she could feel the moisture collecting on her body. In contrast, he looked as cool as a goddamn cucumber. Her irritation with him grew as he crossed his arms over his own chest, making his biceps bulge against his shirt.

"You heard me," he said.

She stalked towards him. "How dare you! I work harder than anyone else in this company."

He didn't reply and her temper, already stretched and frayed, hit the breaking point. She poked him angrily in his hard chest. "What exactly is your problem with me, Mr. Young? Have I done something to offend you? Said something that somehow justifies your poor treatment of me?"

"I'm sure I have no idea what you mean," he said.

"Bullshit!" she spat. "You've been an asshole to me almost from the moment you started working for this company. If you want to fire me, then go ahead and fire me. Or do you prefer to bully people into leaving?"

His eyes, a brilliant shade of dark blue that reminded her of the ocean, narrowed alarmingly and she took a small step back. "It's not my problem if you can't handle a bit of constructive criticism, Ms. Reid."

"It's more than constructive criticism and you know it," she said.

When he remained silent, she shook her head. "You know what? Forget it. There's no point in trying to reason with you."

She turned to storm back to the other side of the elevator. Her arm was grabbed, and she was twisted around and pushed back against the elevator wall. He pinned her body against the wall with his own and cupped the back of her neck.

"What are you doing?" She shoved at his chest and then gasped in a mixture of alarm and excitement when he took her wrists and pinned her arms above her head.

She pulled against his hand, feeling another trickle of excitement in her belly when he tightened his hand around her wrists and held her firmly in place. He looked down at her breasts for a long moment and when he finally glanced back up at her, she almost moaned out loud at the lust in his eyes.

"You have beautiful breasts, Ms. Reid," he murmured. His voice, low and hoarse with desire, brought a shiver to her body. He let his lower body rest against hers and she inhaled sharply when she felt his erection against her hip.

"Complimenting me on my tits isn't going to make up for the fact that you insulted my work abilities," she said.

An adorable grin crossed his face. "My apologies. I happen to think you're excellent at your job and saying you aren't, is a total dick move on my part."

"I – thank you?" she said.

He laughed. "You're welcome."

"Could you please step back, Mr. Young?" She tried to sound authoritative and was dismayed to hear her voice come out in a soft little whisper that practically dripped with need.

"Yes, if that's what you really want. Is it?" he asked.

She didn't reply and he started to release her wrists as he stepped back.

"Wait," she said.

His hand tightened around her wrists again. He lowered his head, and she opened her mouth in anticipation. Instead of kissing her, he bent his head lower and used his warm, wet tongue to lick away the drop of sweat that was sliding down the soft skin of her neck. It was unbelievably erotic, and she released her breath in a long, drawn out hiss.

He nibbled on her jaw and she jerked against him. "Why are you doing this to me?"

"Doing what?" he whispered before sucking her earlobe into his mouth. This time it was impossible to stop the moan from escaping her lips.

"This," she moaned, "you hate me."

"I don't hate you," he murmured. "I find you incredibly attractive and I'm dying to touch you. You don't like this?" He kissed down her neck and chest, nuzzling his face into the crevice between her breasts and licking.

"I – we can't do this," she said.

"But you seem to like it."

For the first time ever, he gave her a full and natural smile, and her damn pussy actually quivered in response.

"It's inappropriate."

"Yes," he agreed, "very inappropriate."

He stared down at her breasts again. "Of course, I've been having inappropriate thoughts about you for a very long time, Ms. Reid."

Before she could wrap her mind around *that* statement, he dipped his head and sucked her lower lip into his mouth. He sucked firmly on it and groaned when her pelvis thrust against him in response. She licked at his upper lip and he pulled his mouth away.

Her eyelids fluttered open and she frowned at him. "Mr. Young, we need -"

"Jason," he said.

She hesitated and then said, "Jason, we -"

Before she could finish, he dipped his head and took her mouth in a hard, punishing kiss. She gasped and he thrust his tongue past her parted lips and deep into her mouth. He explored it roughly, sliding and licking and claiming it as his own until she was weak and trembling.

He released her hands and she immediately slid her hands around his broad shoulders, clinging to him as he continued to kiss her. He moved his hands to her hair and started pulling the pins out.

"Hey!" She pulled her mouth free and tried to slap his hands away from her hair. Her hair tended to poof up, especially in the heat, and she wasn't interested in having him see her messy, unruly hair.

He swung her around, pushing her chest against the elevator wall. He continued to pull the pins out of her hair, shoving them into his pocket. She squirmed and twisted. The metal bar that ran around the elevator wall was digging into her abdomen and she shoved her ass against him, trying to use her weight to gain some breathing room.

It had the wrong effect. As soon as he felt her soft bottom press up against his erection, he groaned in her ear and pinned her even more heavily against the wall. He ground his cock against her ass as he pulled the last of the hair pins free, and her hair tumbled halfway down her back in soft, damp waves.

He gathered her hair into his fists and tugged on it before dropping his face into the silky strands and inhaling. He inhaled once more before gathering it into a loose ponytail in one fist and tugging her head back.

He slipped his other arm around her waist and kissed the side of her neck. "I like your hair, Ms. Reid."

"Thank you," she moaned as he licked the sensitive spot below her earlobe.

"I want you to wear it down at the office from now on," he demanded.

"No." She would have shaken her head, but he was still holding her hair in a firm grip and she couldn't move it.

"Yes," he said.

"You can't tell me -" Her protest turned into a groan of pleasure when he released her hair, slid both arms around her and cupped her breasts through her blouse.

He looked down over her shoulder as he kneaded her breasts, rubbing her tight nipples with his thumbs. Her head fell back on his shoulder and she arched her back, pushing more of her breasts into his hands. He unbuttoned her shirt and yanked it down her arms. As soon as it was free and tossed to the floor, he pressed himself back against her.

## CHAPTER 2

J ason was almost frantic with need as he unbuttoned Lucy's shirt and pulled it off. He threw it on the floor and pressed his chest against her back. Lucy was always so cool to him, always so polite and distant with a sense of control to her that he admired. Now, watching her face flush with desire and feeling her ass grind against him, he was determined to break that control. He wanted to see her naked, wanted to hear her moaning his name as he made her come repeatedly.

She was wearing a white demi-bra. The tops of her breasts overflowed the short cups and he groaned at the sight of her pale, luscious flesh. He had intended to tease her for a few moments, to touch her through her bra until she was begging him to take it off of her, but he couldn't wait. He released the clasp of her bra with a practiced flick and raked the straps down her arms.

"Jason, wait!" She brought her arms up, keeping the cups of her bra on her breasts. "There'll be cameras. What if someone's watching us?"

"Power failure, remember?" He tugged her arms away

from her breasts. "No one's watching. And if they are, who cares? Who wouldn't want to watch a beautiful woman being fucked until she comes so hard, she screams?"

She swallowed hard. "I'm not going to fuck you, Jason."

"Why not?"

He was genuinely curious, and she tilted her head to look at him. "Because you're my boss, remember? What if the other employees found out?"

"I won't tell them if you won't." He dropped his mouth to hers again. His tongue pushed at her closed lips and, with a helpless moan, she opened them. He coaxed her tongue into his mouth and then sucked on it as he pulled her bra free. He added it to the growing pile of clothes on the elevator floor.

He released her mouth and drew in a short, harsh breath. "Oh my God."

Her breasts were more glorious than he could have ever imagined. They were round and full and despite their large size, deliciously perky. Her nipples were rose coloured and hard as pearls.

With slightly trembling hands, he cupped them and rolled her nipples between his fingers and thumbs. He pulled and tugged on them until the rose colour had deepened and she was gasping and pushing her ass mindlessly against his cock.

His cock was swelling in his pants and his balls tightening until he wasn't entirely sure he could stop from coming in his pants. He had fantasized for months about seeing Lucy naked and pleading for his touch, but actually seeing her like this was turning him on in ways he couldn't explain. He pinched her nipples to see her reaction and growled with satisfaction when it made her moan even louder and arch her back. Her nipples were practically begging for his mouth, and he whirled her around and bent down before sucking the left one into his mouth.

LUCY FORGOT TO BREATHE WHEN JASON SUCKED HER LEFT nipple into his mouth. He flicked the sensitive bud with the tip of his tongue before suckling hard on it. She sucked in a breath of air and curled her fingers into his thick hair, urging his mouth to her right breast. He let her guide his mouth and sucked and nipped at her right nipple until she was gasping and crying out.

"Your breasts are incredible." He kissed her on the mouth again and she reached for his shirt buttons, suddenly anxious to see his naked chest. His shirt was soaked with sweat, and he helped her peel it off.

She took another deep, shuddering breath. She knew he was in good shape. Even in his expensive suits it was easy to tell that he was a man who worked out, but she hadn't imagined the six-pack she was now seeing. Unlike the guys at her gym who waxed and shaved their chests smooth, his chest and abdomen were deeply tanned and covered in a layer of dark hair.

She reached out and traced his abs with the tip of her finger, enjoying the sharp inhale he made at her touch.

"How are you so tanned?" she said.

He grinned at her. "Beach volleyball."

She let her fingers slide up his chest, circling her finger around one flat nipple and giving her own smile of satisfaction when he jerked against her. He pulled her forward until her breasts were brushing against his chest and reached around to squeeze her ample ass through her skirt.

She wiggled her hand between their bodies and boldly slipped it into his pants. He tensed against her as she pushed her fingers under the waistband of his briefs and wrapped her fingers around his large cock.

"Fuck," he moaned as she moved her hand with long, firm strokes. He threw his head back, his hands squeezing her ass so tightly she was positive she would have bruises on it in the morning.

He grabbed the zipper at the back of her skirt and yanked it down. Before she could stop him, he was tugging her skirt down. It pooled around her ankles and he stared at her body. She was wearing a plain white thong and, feeling shy, she pulled her hand free of his pants and reached for her skirt.

He shook his head and pinned her hands down at her sides. "No, don't do that." He drank in the sight of her pale flesh, his eyes traveling over her breasts, the curve of her stomach and her long bare legs.

He kissed her again, their tongues tangling together as he shoved his leg between hers, forcing her thighs apart so that he could slip his hand between them. He cupped her pussy, touching her heat and wetness through the thin material of her panties.

He pushed his hand into her panties, slid his fingers past her soft curls and thrust two of them deep inside of her slick pussy. She tore her mouth from his, crying out when he slid his fingers in and out of her. Her knees were beginning to shake, and the pleasure built in the pit of her stomach. Her pelvis throbbed and ached with need and she arched her back as the release she was looking for drew closer.

"Oh please," she moaned when he abruptly stopped moving his fingers.

"Please what, pretty little Lucy?" he whispered in her ear.

She shuddered when he called her Lucy for the first time, liking the sound of her name on his tongue.

"Please what?" he repeated.

"Please, Jason. Make me come," she begged.

She clung to him, her breasts flattened against his chest

and her hard nipples poking into him. When he pushed at her leg with his, she spread her thighs wide and reached between them, grabbing at his hand and trying to make him move it against her. He refused and Lucy caught a glimpse of his look of satisfaction.

She blushed furiously. His mouth and fingers had made her so hot, so ready to come, that she couldn't think straight. Just the touch of his rough fingers against her pussy was sending shockwaves of pleasure down her legs, and she was dangerously close to coming.

It was happening exactly like she had feared it would. He was making her lose the control she was always so proud of, and she could feel the embarrassment creeping in past her fog of lust. She had never begged a man to make her come before. *They* begged her and that was the way it was supposed to be.

She closed her eyes and counted backward from one hundred, forcing herself to come back from the brink. She didn't want to lose control, she told herself. She hated losing control. Her body vehemently disagreed with her, but she ignored it fiercely.

She tried to slip her hand into his pants again, she would have him begging to come if it was the last thing she did, but he shook his head and grabbed both her wrists in one strong hand. He pinned them above her head once more.

"Let me go." She yanked fruitlessly at his hard grip.

He grinned. "Really? A minute ago, you were begging me to make you come and now you want me to let you go?"

She flushed again. She was angry now and she had forgotten that he still had two fingers deep inside of her.

"I've changed my mind," she lied.

"That's too bad," he said. "I haven't even had the chance to touch your clit yet."

He parted the wet lips of her pussy with his thumb and found her hard and swollen clit. He pressed on it with the pad of his thumb, and she bit back the moan of pleasure that was trying to escape.

He withdrew his fingers but continued to rub and circle her clit. He bent his head and took one of her nipples into his mouth again. He sucked gently, then firmly, then gently again as she moaned and arched her back and rocked her pelvis against his hand.

The overwhelming need was back, making her forget her intentions to have him begging. It raged like a hot fire inside of her, and she was helpless to stop the small moans and whimpers from escaping her lips. Still holding her hands captive above her head, he moved his mouth to her ear.

He traced the curve of it with his tongue before whispering, "Do you still want to come, pretty little Lucy?"

"Yes," she moaned.

He stopped moving his thumb against her swollen clit. "Are you sure?"

"Yes, please!" she gasped out. "Please, I want to come." She moved her pelvis frantically against him.

He chuckled with satisfaction, a low, warm sound that should have made her angry but instead sent another wave of pleasure through her lower body.

Lucy couldn't breathe. She was standing on the edge, every nerve on fire and every muscle taut with expectation. She had lost control completely, was at the mercy of his touch, and she loved it. She knew in that moment that whatever he asked her to do she would do without hesitating. Even as her mind rebelled at the foreign thought, her body was basking in it.

He kissed her and moved his fingers against her clit. She came immediately, screaming her pleasure into his mouth as her body shook violently against his. She leaned against the wall of the elevator with her legs trembling. He was still cupping her pussy and he caressed her heated skin again before slipping his fingers free. She watched as he put his index finger into his mouth and sucked it clean of her juices.

"You taste so sweet, little Lucy," he said. She was surprised to feel another bolt of heat run down her legs.

His fingers gripped the waistband of her panties. He tugged them down her legs, kneeling at her feet and helping her to step out of them. She kicked her shoes off and frowned a little when, instead of dropping her panties on the floor with the rest of her clothes, he stuffed them into his pants pocket.

"I want those back."

"Of course." He reached for his belt buckle. "But first, I'm going to fuck you."

She swallowed hard as he undid his belt and the button on his pants before reaching into his back pocket. He pulled a condom from his wallet. Quickly he unzipped his pants but didn't bother taking off his pants and underwear. He simply pulled his cock free, glancing up at her sharp inhale.

LUCY WAS STARING AT HIS LARGE COCK WITH A HUNGRY LOOK on her face. For a moment, Jason was tempted to push her to her knees and make her suck his cock. He ignored his urge. If she surrounded him with her wet, hot mouth, he'd lose control. He was already close to coming and he wanted to be inside of her when that happened. He wanted to know how tight her pussy was and feel her inner muscles grip his cock. He ripped open the condom package and smoothed on the thin rubber.

He pulled her into his arms again and kissed her hard on

the mouth. His cock rubbed against the soft skin of her belly and he groaned, trying to keep himself from exploding all over her. He needed to fuck her, and he needed to do it right now.

"Against the wall or on the floor?" he said into her ear.

"I... what?" she said as he cupped her breast and pinched her nipple.

"Do you want to be fucked against the wall or on the floor?" he said.

"I don't..." She was blushing hotly, and he made the decision for her.

"The floor then."

It was his preference anyway. He wanted to be on top of her for their first time. He wanted to have those long legs spread wide around him. He wanted to watch her writhe under him, moaning and coming as he fucked her.

He pulled her down to the floor, pushing her onto her back and kneeling between her legs. He grabbed one thigh with his hand and hooked it around his waist. He pushed the head of his cock against her wet entrance and they both moaned.

"Jason, please," she moaned breathlessly.

He thrust the head of his cock into her before groaning. "Fuck, Lucy. You're so fucking tight."

"Please, oh please," she whimpered. Her hands scrabbled for purchase on the tile floor as she arched her hips upward.

He responded by sliding further into her. He stopped, waiting as she stretched around him, until with one final push he slid his entire cock into her warm wetness. She stared up at him, her mouth open and her eyes dark with lust as she tried to adjust to his size.

He waited. Every muscle in his body screamed at him to

move and his cock throbbed inside of her, but he waited. Finally, his voice hoarse, he asked, "Ready?"

"Yes," she moaned and then made a loud cry of pleasure when he immediately began to plunge in and out of her.

She bent her knees and planted her feet on the slick tile of the elevator floor as he propped himself above her on his hands. He thrust roughly in and out of her of her wet, hot pussy. She ran her fingers over his flat stomach, smiling when he groaned and jerked against her. She slid her hands around his waist and clung to him as he rocked above her.

"So thick," she moaned.

"Wrap your legs around my waist," he demanded.

She obeyed, hooking her feet together in the small of his back. He groaned as the new position made her pussy tighten around his cock. She rose up to meet him, her hips slapping against his as he bent his head and took her nipple into his mouth. He sucked hard on it and she arched her back, her hands digging into the smooth, hard flesh of his back.

"Jason, oh Jason," she whimpered.

She was starting to lose the easy, natural rhythm they had fallen into as her pleasure grew. He looked down at her and sucked in his breath. Her long dark hair was spread out underneath her, her pale skin flushed with pleasure, and her nipples hard and wet from his mouth. Her entire body glistened with moisture, and her pussy was soaking wet around his cock.

She moaned his name repeatedly, and just the sound of her soft voice saying his name brought him closer and closer to the edge. His balls tightening, he thrust wildly into her. She gave another loud cry of delight before she stiffened underneath him and her nails dug painfully into his back. He echoed her cry when he felt the muscles of her pussy tighten around his cock and a flood of wetness.

He thrust twice more and then came, his hips slamming into hers and his entire body shaking as his orgasm roared through him. He collapsed against her soft body, burying his face in her neck and panting harshly.

After a few moments, he lifted his upper body from hers and stared down at her for so long that she blushed. "What?"

"Jesus, Lucy. You have no idea how -"

The lights suddenly flickered on, bathing them in brightness, and the elevator lurched before continuing its smooth descent.

"Shit!" He pushed away from her, grabbed her hand, and hauled her to her feet. He pulled off the condom, tying it closed and shoving it into the pocket of his pants. Beside him, Lucy yanked up her skirt and zipped it. As he pulled his shirt on, cursing under his breath when it stuck to his sweaty skin, Lucy struggled into her bra.

"What floor?" she said.

He glanced upward. "Tenth." He looked down at the front of his pants. Lucy's juices had soaked the front of them while he was fucking her, and he groaned silently at the large wet spot.

---

Trying not to panic, Lucy yanked her bra straps up. "Goddammit!"

The straps were twisted and digging into her skin, but she ignored them and threw her shirt on. Her hands refused to work the buttons properly and she cursed again. She buttoned the top three and struggled into her suit jacket, hurriedly doing up the buttons on it and shoving her feet into her shoes. She snagged her purse from the floor as the elevator shuddered to a stop and made a quiet dinging noise.

She glanced at Jason. He had his suit jacket draped over his arm so that it covered the front of his pants, and she was irritated at how calm he looked.

"Give me my panties!" she hissed at him.

He grinned at her. "Too late now, little Lucy."

The doors opened and Lucy had time for a quick prayer that the parking garage would be empty before the two maintenance men appeared before them. They were large and burly men with grease-stained coveralls and hands.

"Sorry about that folks!" the one said cheerfully.

"No problem." Jason cleared his throat and put his hand on the small of Lucy's back, ushering her out of the elevator.

The second maintenance man stared at her for so long that dull heat invaded her cheeks. She risked a glance downward, sighing with relief when her clothing appeared straight and nothing was hanging out.

Jason pushed her forward and she gave the men a tiny, embarrassed nod as they walked away. She passed a large SUV and stumbled to a stop when she caught a glimpse of her reflection in the tinted rear-view window.

She stared horrified at her reflection. Her face and throat were covered in red marks from Jason's stubble, and her lips were swollen from his hard mouth. But it was her dark hair that revealed their activity in the elevator. It surrounded her face in a huge halo. It was the most spectacular 'just been fucked' hair she'd ever seen. Her hair and the combination of her face and mouth made her look like she had stumbled off a porno set.

"Excuse me, sir!" Jason turned back as the first maintenance man entered the elevator and picked up something from the floor. "Is this your wallet then?"

"Yes, thanks very much," Jason replied as he stepped back into the elevator.

"Sorry again for the inconvenience." The man dropped a wink at him, and Jason had the good grace to flush as Lucy thought about bolting to her car. The man could obviously smell the musky scent of their coupling and, if he couldn't, one look at her hair and he'd have to be an idiot not to know.

When Jason rejoined her, she nodded briefly. "Good night, Mr. Young."

"Lucy, wait."

"I have to go." She hurried to her car, slid inside and drove out of the garage without looking at him.

---

NODDING ONCE MORE TO THE MAINTENANCE MEN, JASON walked to his own car. He slid behind the wheel before starting the car and turning the air conditioner on full blast. He let the cold air cool his sweaty skin as he stared blankly out the windshield. He'd hoped to convince Lucy to come back to his place for a cool shower and a bite to eat before coaxing her into his bed, and he was disappointed that she ran off so quickly.

He closed his eyes for a moment, imagining how Lucy would look lying naked in his king-size bed. Just picturing her pale flesh was giving him an erection again. He fished in his pocket and brought out the scrap of white cotton that was her underwear. He stared at them for a long moment before smiling and placing them back in his pocket. She couldn't avoid him forever. She'd have to ask for her panties back eventually.

# CHAPTER 3

L ucy was almost to her office when she felt the strap go. She rolled her eyes in irritation and veered away from her office toward the washroom. She should have known better than to wear this particular bra. It was one of her older ones and she knew the strap was starting to wear. It didn't seem to matter how expensive the bra was, eventually the weight of her breasts put too much strain on the material, and she ended up with busted underwire or torn straps.

She ducked into the washroom and stripped off her suit jacket. It was the one Friday of the month where they were allowed to wear casual clothes. Today she had paired her usual jacket with a thin, white cotton camisole and a knee-length jean skirt. Calf-hugging leather boots completed the outfit.

Cursing under her breath, she dug through her purse for a safety pin as Penny, one of the admin staff, came barging in.

"Whatcha' doin'?" she asked as she checked her makeup in the mirror.

"My stupid bra strap broke," Lucy grumbled. She gave a snort of triumph as she found a safety pin deep in the bottom of her purse. "Can you help me with this? The strap ripped at the back. Can you pin it back on?"

"Sure."

Penny smoothed the strap of her bra down and pulled it tight before carefully pinning it together. She stepped back. "There you go, Lucy-Lou. Good as new."

There was a soft ping as the safety pin bent under the pressure and popped open.

"Dammit!" Lucy snapped as the sharp end of the pin dragged across her soft flesh. Penny untangled the pin and dropped it in the garbage can. "Hold on, I might have another one."

Before she could start digging through her purse again, Penny laughed. "Forget it, Lucy. A safety pin is no match for your boobs."

Lucy sighed and stared at herself in the mirror. "I guess I can make it through the day like this."

Penny shook her head. "It'll look better if you just take off the damn thing."

"Are you crazy? I can't go without a bra in the office."

"What's the big deal? You're young, they're perky, and you're wearing a suit jacket. No one will notice. Take it off and we'll see what it looks like."

Lucy unhooked her bra, yanked it out from under her camisole, and dropped it on the counter. She studied her upper body in the mirror. The camisole she was wearing was a bit too small but that was working in her favour. She walked in place for a few minutes. Her breasts jiggled a little more than usual, but the suit jacket would cover that up.

"Well, as long as you don't run, I think you'll be okay." Penny grinned.

As Lucy slipped into her suit jacket and buttoned it up, Penny sighed and cupped her own small breasts. "Jesus, I wish I had your tits. I swear to God they're perkier than mine."

Lucy rolled her eyes. "They're not always a blessing, Penny. Trust me."

Penny turned sideways and straightened her back, staring critically at herself. "Yeah, but I bet if I had tits like yours, I could bed Jason Young and win the damn office bet before the day was over."

Lucy flushed a little. It was a week and she still couldn't believe what had happened while she was trapped in the elevator with Jason during the power outage. She would be inclined to believe it was a dream if not for the fading marks on her breasts from Jason's mouth. Not to mention the vivid memory of how amazing it felt when Jason had lowered her to the elevator floor, spread her legs wide, and fucked her to a mind-blowing orgasm.

She turned and stuffed her bra into the garbage can. Remembering what happened with Jason was a bad idea.

"Alex says he's a boob man. She says she's caught him twice staring at her tits," Penny snorted. "Of course, Alex says every man stares at her tits, even Paul, and he's got a goddamn boyfriend. Besides, it'd be difficult for our new boss not to stare at them – she shoves them in his face every chance she gets."

She glanced at Lucy who was very studiously examining a loose thread on her jacket. "Figured out yet why he seems to hate you?"

"Nope and I don't really care."

"It doesn't bother you at all?" Penny asked.

"Why would it?" Lucy shrugged. "As long as he thinks I'm good at my job, why should I care if he likes me or not?"

"I guess. Personally, I would love to get to know him better. The man is smart, gorgeous, and has a voice like warm honey. He practically drips sex. God, what I wouldn't give to see him naked – just once."

Lucy blushed as an image of Jason's naked chest flashed into her head. Just thinking about him naked made her pulse race and her lower body ache. She shook her head. It was a one-time thing, a momentary lapse in her judgment, and there was no point reliving it. She wouldn't see him naked again. She abruptly grabbed her purse and headed for the door.

Penny frowned. "You okay, Luce?"

"Fine." She forced herself to smile at the petite blonde. "I'll see you at lunch."

She left the bathroom and walked down the hallway. About five feet in front of her, the door to Jerry's office opened and Jason stepped out into the hallway. Lucy immediately ducked into the small room that held the photocopier and five large metal filing cabinets. She eased the door shut behind her and hid behind the last and largest of the filing cabinets.

In the week since she'd let Jason fuck her in the elevator, she'd managed to successfully avoid seeing or talking to him. Considering the small size of their office, it was a rather impressive feat. She closed her eyes and held her breath, praying that he hadn't seen her and ignoring the small voice that called her a coward.

There was a soft click. She tilted her head, straining to hear over the loud hum of the photocopier. Was that the door? After a minute she released her breath in a harsh rush. It was nothing. A few more minutes and she could sneak to her office, close the door and –

"Do you often hide in here, Ms. Reid?"

She shrieked softly in alarm, her eyes popping open and her whole body jerking wildly. She winced as the back of her head bounced off the hard filing cabinet.

"You scared the hell out of me!" She glared at Jason who was standing in front of her looking ridiculously sexy in a dark blue t-shirt and faded jeans.

"Sorry," he replied, not sounding sorry at all.

"Excuse me. I have work to do," she said.

Before she could duck around him, he planted his hands against the filing cabinet on either side of her head and blocked her exit.

"You've been avoiding me." His voice was low and sexy, and an involuntary shudder went through her.

"No, I haven't," she lied. "I've had a very busy week."

"Oh really? So, you didn't duck in here and hide behind this filing cabinet when you saw me in the hallway?" He leaned closer and dipped his head until his nose was nearly buried in her neck. He inhaled deeply as she cleared her throat.

"No. I was, uh, looking for something." Her voice was a nervous squeak.

"You smell good," he said.

"Thank you."

He smiled at her. "I've thought about you all week, you know. Thought about what it was like to kiss you, how turned on it made me when you moaned, and how beautiful your breasts are."

He leaned forward and kissed her jaw right below her ear. "I thought about how good it felt to fuck your tight, little pussy."

She moaned and turned her head, capturing his mouth with hers. He opened his mouth as she thrust her tongue between his lips and gripped his head, holding him steady as she explored his mouth.

He pressed her up against the filing cabinet and kissed her. She barely noticed his long fingers undoing the buttons on her suit jacket until he had pushed it open. His gaze widened when he saw her chest.

"Well, Ms. Reid. You take casual Fridays to a whole different level, don't you?" He gave her a wicked grin, and she blushed to the roots of her hair.

"My bra strap broke. I didn't have a choice," she said.

"Oh, I'm not complaining. Believe me." He grinned again at her.

She suddenly stiffened. "Did you hear something?"

She strained to look around him. She could have sworn she heard the door again. She pushed away from the filing cabinet and then moaned as his hot, wet mouth closed around one nipple. He sucked hard on it through the thin material of her camisole, and she fell back against the filing cabinet as he lightly bit her nipple.

"Mr. Young, stop," she said.

He released her nipple and she stared down at her chest. Her nipple was rock hard and straining against the wet spot his mouth had left on her camisole. As she watched, he reached out with one long finger and lazily brushed circles around her tight nipple.

"Oh, Jesus. We need to stop." She brought her hands up and covered both her breasts. He hadn't even touched the left one, but her nipple was just as hard as the right. It poked into the palm of her hand like a hard button.

"Why?" He licked her collarbone with the tip of his tongue as he pressed his erection against her.

"Because someone could come in! Because this isn't appropriate! Because my ass could get fired for fucking you!" she said.

"If anyone gets fired for us fucking, it'll be me," he said with a small grin.

"This isn't funny!" She glared at him. "Look, what

happened in the elevator was a momentary lapse in judgment, that's all. I lost control for a few minutes and -"

"You seemed to enjoy losing control," he replied. "In fact, if I remember correctly, there was quite a bit of begging."

"I didn't beg -"

"You did too," he said.

He rubbed her abdomen through the camisole before placing his mouth to her ear. "Please, Jason. Please make me come," he mimicked her in his low voice.

She took a deep breath. "Mr. Young, listen -"

"I liked it when you begged," he said. "I liked hearing you moaning my name and pleading with me to make you come. Be honest, you liked it too didn't you?"

She swallowed hard and stared into his eyes. "Yes."

He stared at her mouth with barely concealed lust and her lips parted in response.

"Do you know how hard it makes me when I can just look at you and your mouth opens like that?" His gaze flickered downward. "I love how hard your nipples go when I touch them, and I love how unbelievably wet your pussy gets."

He reached down and traced her bare knee. "Is your pussy wet right now, pretty Lucy?"

"N-no," she said.

He chuckled. "I think you're lying. And I think you're lying on purpose because you know I'll check for myself. You want my fingers in your pussy again. Don't you, sweet Lucy?"

His hand started to inch under her skirt, and she sighed in defeat. "Yes. Touch me, Jason. Please."

He smiled in triumph and leaned in to kiss her.

"Then I told him that if he wanted the damn letter typed, he could do it himself or ask Penny. I'm not a goddamn secretary."

They both froze as the door opened and Alex's voice drifted in. "It's bad enough that I have to do my own photo-copying. Seriously, what does that bitch Penny do all day, other than try to get Jason to notice her?"

"Who isn't trying to get Jason to notice them?" Maureen from accounting said dryly.

"Lucy isn't," Alex replied. "Of course, it's because she knows she doesn't have a chance with him."

There was muted beeping as she punched the buttons on the photocopier. She raised her voice to be heard over the whir of the machine. "She needs to get her fat ass to a gym for Christ's sake."

Jason's face reddened with anger and Lucy watched in alarm as he started to push away from her. She grabbed his arms and yanked him back toward her, shaking her head fran-tically. She rolled her eyes and mouthed, "I don't care."

He frowned down at her as Alex sighed. "I've got to step up my game with him. I'm going to win that bet if it's the last thing I do."

Maureen laughed. "Yeah - you, me and all the other women in the office."

Jason cocked his eyebrow at her and mouthed, "Bet?"

She shrugged and widened her eyes innocently as Alex stapled her sheets of paper together. "Sorry, Maureen, but when Jason sees what I'm wearing today, he'll be begging me to sleep with him."

Jason mimed retching. It was such an unexpected depar-ture from his usual professional manner that Lucy snorted soft laughter. She clapped her hand over her mouth and glared at him.

"Did you hear that?" Alex asked.

"Hear what?"

"Nothing, I guess," Alex said.

Lucy sagged against the filing cabinet with relief as the door opened and the two women left the room.

Jason grinned at her. "Well, that was a close one."

"Too close," she said. "This is why we can't do this. If the others find out..."

She pushed free of him, buttoning her suit jacket and hurrying toward the door.

She glanced back at him as she reached for the door handle. "This is a bad idea, Jason, and you know it."

He smiled at her. "What can I say, I'm a bad boy."

She rolled her eyes as he said, "Are you sure you don't want to come back here for a few minutes? I bet I can use my mouth to make you come in less than three minutes."

She hesitated as a vision of his dark head nestled between her legs went through her.

He grinned again. "You're picturing it, aren't you?"

"No!" She opened the door, took a quick glance both ways, and practically ran to her office. She shut the door and leaned back against it, taking deep, calming breaths.

She slapped herself on the leg. She had never wanted to punch someone as much as she did Jason Young. He was driving her insane. It'd be easy enough. Sure, he was big and strong but knock his legs out from under him and she could pin him to the ground. Then it would just be a matter of punching him in the face.

She closed her eyes, the small grin dropping from her face when her mind presented her not with an image of punching Jason in the face, but an image of her riding his hard cock. She pressed her thighs together as her pussy throbbed and dampened in response. She was already wet from being so close to him in the filing room. If she kept up this kind of thinking, she'd ruin her damn underwear.

# CHAPTER 4

Lucy didn't turn at the soft knock on her door. Her desk faced the window not the door, but she didn't need to turn around to know who had entered the room. "I know, Elliot. Mr. Young is waiting. Tell him I'll have the damn file to him in five minutes. I want one final look at it."

"Actually, I thought I would look at it while you were finishing up with it - just to expedite the process." Jason's deep voice spoke beside her and she glanced upward, groaning inwardly.

"I need five minutes," she mumbled.

"No problem." He rested his hand on the back of her chair and started to read the screen. "We'll look at it together."

Lucy swallowed nervously. Jason was standing too close. He smelled delicious and she imagined that she could almost feel the heat from his body. His crotch was right beside her head and she kept stealing glances at it and licking her lips. She wondered what he would do if she reached out and unzipped his jeans. What he would say if she pulled his cock out and wrapped her lips around it. She took another quick look as her nipples tightened, and her mouth went dry.

Suddenly it didn't seem to matter that her office door was wide open or that just earlier this morning she had told him it was a bad idea. The thought of sucking his cock was heating her up and making her tingle with anticipation. She had to squeeze the arms of her chair to stop herself from reaching for his zipper.

"Ms. Reid, if you keep looking at my crotch and licking your lips, I'm going to unzip my pants right here," Jason said without taking his eyes off the screen. "I don't think I have to tell you what will happen next."

Her stomach clenched with pleasure and she whipped her head back to the computer screen in front of her, willing herself not to lick her lips again.

She had wrangled her thick hair into a ponytail this morning and he capture the end of it, pulling until she was forced to look up at him. "Unless, of course, you want me to unzip my pants? Just say the word and I'll do it, Lucy."

Still holding her ponytail in one hand, he traced her mouth with the index finger of his other one. He pushed and she parted her lips so he could slip the tip of his finger inside her warm, wet mouth. She closed her lips around his finger and sucked hard.

"Jesus," he muttered.

He let her suck for a few seconds, closing his eyes and groaning when she tipped her head forward and took his entire finger into her mouth. She moved her mouth back and forth along his finger, rubbing her tongue around it and sucking eagerly. For a moment, his hand tightened almost painfully in her hair, and then he was pulling his finger free and releasing his grip on her hair. He kept his eyes closed for a moment, panting harshly in her quiet office, before finally looking at her.

Her face red, she stared at him in horror. "I'm so sorry,

Jason. I shouldn't have done that. That was really, um, inappropriate."

"I started it," he rasped.

He took a deep breath as she cleared her throat. "We need to finish this file."

"Right, the file." His voice was still hoarse, and he grimaced as he bent down and looked back at the screen. "So far it seems to be looking good."

His head was right next to hers and she could feel his warm breath on her cheek. She inhaled when his right hand slipped into the top of her jacket and under her camisole. He cupped her naked breast, squeezing it roughly before rubbing her nipple between his thumb and finger.

"Jason," she moaned.

"I'm sorry. I can't seem to keep my hands off of you." Despite his apology, he continued to touch her, and she closed her eyes as pleasure drenched her insides.

"Keep reading, Ms. Reid," he instructed. "We have a deadline, remember?"

She dragged her gaze back to the screen. The words were meaningless, but she struggled to look for errors as the tips of his fingers explored the hollow between her breasts. He cupped her other breast, teasing the nipple with his fingers until it hardened into a stiff peak.

"I highly approve of you going braless, little Lucy. It makes it so much easier to see how delightfully responsive your breasts are to my touch."

He pinched her nipple hard and she gave a small squeak of need, her back arching helplessly.

"Hmm," he whispered, "you don't seem to be finishing up this file as quickly as you promised. What should I do about that?"

He pulled on one nipple and then the other as Lucy

squeezed the arms of the chair and pressed her mouth closed. Whimpers of need were threatening to escape as he rubbed and touched and kneaded her full breasts.

"Mr. Young?"

With his body and Lucy's chair hiding his arm and hand, he continued to slowly rub her nipple as he looked behind him. "What is it, Alex?"

"Mr. Hanson is looking for you."

Lucy took a quick glance at Alex. She leaned in the doorway, one hand on the hip of her skin-tight jeans and the other playing with the low-cut opening of her blouse. "He's wondering where the file is?"

"Ms. Reid and I were just finishing it," he said.

He glanced down at Lucy's flushed face and pulled hard on her nipple. "Ms. Reid, have you finished?"

"Yes," she squeaked out.

"Good. Email it to me please." He glanced at the doorway, his gaze narrowing when he saw Alex still standing there. "Is there something else, Alex?"

"Um, no." Lucy could almost hear Alex's smile falling off her face.

"Good, then you're dismissed."

She left and Jason waited a beat before saying, "I want to invite you to my house tonight for drinks, Lucy."

She stared at him and he smiled encouragingly. "My house is right on the beach. We can relax on the deck and watch the sunset. What do you think?"

"Mr. Young, that's very nice of you but -"

He was still cupping her breast in his hand and rubbing her nipple with his thumb. It was making it extremely difficult to concentrate. She put her hand over his, stilling his movements.

"That's nice of you to invite me to your home but I think
-"

"Don't answer right away." He gave her breast a final squeeze and straightened. "Think about it and you can let me know by the end of the day." He left her office without giving her a chance to reply.

---

LUCY STRETCHED AND GLANCED AT HER WATCH. IT WAS THREE o'clock. She had two hours left before she had to give Jason her answer. She drummed her fingers on her bottom lip. A part of her - a very big part of her - wanted to say yes. She wanted to go to his house, have a glass of wine, and let Jason do whatever he wanted to her. Her common sense, however, wouldn't stop arguing with her about it.

*He's your boss! What if you get caught? What if after a few nights of mind-blowing sex, you get tired of him or he gets tired of you? How awkward will it be at work then? And what if your coworkers find out? Do you really want to be known as the girl in the office who's banging the boss?*

*You would get a nice weekend spa trip.*

She groaned and rested her elbows on her desk, burying her head in her hands. What she was thinking was madness. She could not, under any circumstance, go to Jason Young's house. If she even considered –

"Lucy?"

The intercom on her phone buzzed and she twitched in surprise.

"Hi, Jerry. What's up?"

"Can you come to Jason's office please? We have an issue we'd like to discuss with you."

"Of course." Lucy jumped up, her heart banging nervously in her chest.

*Oh shit. They'd been found out already.*

She hurried down the hallway and skidded to a stop in front of the closed door of Jason's office. Her heart still knocking painfully against her breastbone, she raised her hand and rapped on the door.

"Come in."

She entered the room, her stomach dropping to her feet at the serious looks on the two men's faces. She walked across the room, her knees shaking and her hands clammy with sweat. "Is there something wrong?"

"As a matter of fact, there is," Jerry said. "Have a seat."

He indicated the chair next to him and Lucy sat down numbly. She stole a quick look at Jason. She couldn't read the look on his face and she turned back to Jerry when he cleared his throat.

"Lucy -"

Jason's intercom buzzed and Carol said, "Mr. Young? Is Mr. Hanson there with you?"

"I am," Jerry said.

"Your wife is on line three. Your hot water tank is leaking all over the basement. She wants to speak to you immediately."

"Well, shit." Jerry scowled and stood up. "I gotta go." He glanced at Jason. "Should we wait until Monday?"

"No, I'll speak with Ms. Reid on my own. Have a good weekend, Jerry."

"Oh, I doubt that now." He nodded distractedly and left, shutting the door behind him.

Lucy squeezed her hands together and stared straight ahead as Jason stood and walked across the room. He locked the door and returned to his desk. He stared thoughtfully at her as he sat in his chair. "Have you thought about my proposal for tonight, Ms. Reid?"

She stared at him. "What?"

"My proposal. Will you be joining me for drinks tonight?"

Her mouth dropped open. "I'm about to be fired for sleeping with you, and you want to know if I'll be dropping by for drinks at your stupid beach house?"

He frowned. "You're not being fired."

"Then why am I here?"

"I'll get to that in a minute," he replied. "Are you coming by tonight?"

"No, I'm not," she said. "Thank you for the invitation but I'm afraid I'll have to decline."

"Okay." He shrugged and looked at his computer screen. A ripple of hurt went through her at his easy dismissal of her and she told herself not to be an idiot. It was what she wanted after all.

"There was an issue with the file you reviewed this morning for uploading," Jason said.

"What was wrong with it? Is it something serious? Did it get uploaded to the website with the mistake?" Her heart, which was just starting to slow down, sped up again.

"It did, and it was serious enough," he said. "Why don't you come around and look?"

She stood and walked around the desk before bending and staring at his screen. She searched the article frantically. She hated making mistakes in her work.

"Do you see it, Ms. Reid?" Jason's voice washed over her while his hand slipped under her skirt and stroked her thigh.

She gasped and clamped her legs together. "Not yet."

"Keep looking." He ran his fingers over the sensitive skin on the back of her knee and she trembled wildly.

"You have the softest skin, Ms. Reid. Did you know that?" Jason said.

"No," she said.

"You do. Have you found the mistake yet?"

"No, stop distracting me."

"You know, I've always thought the sign of a good copy editor is their ability to work well under extreme pressure or distraction as you like to call it."

She could hear the laughter in his voice as he ran his fingers along the outside of her thigh before trailing them back down to her knees. He pushed his hand between her knees.

"Spread your legs, Lucy," he demanded.

"No."

He leaned forward and bit her playfully on the ass through her jean skirt, making her gasp and jump. "Pretty please?"

He squeezed her ass with one hand, and she groaned and shifted her feet apart.

"That's my good girl." He let his fingers dance up her inner thigh. "Are you still looking for that mistake?"

"Yes," she gritted out as he slipped his hand up to her ass.

"Good, keep looking." He caressed her naked ass cheeks. "A thong again? I do like your choice of panties, Ms. Reid."

"You need to give me the other pair back."

"Do I have a pair of your panties?" he asked innocently.

"You know damn well that you do." She jerked when his finger pulled on the string between her ass cheeks.

"You're supposed to be looking for your mistake," he said.

She turned back to the screen as he moved his hand between her thighs. He traced her inner thigh, and she made another moan of need when he traced the curve where her thigh met her pussy. He let his fingers skate over the damp material of her panties, almost but not quite touching her. She sighed with frustration and widened her thighs a little more.

"The mistake, Ms. Reid," he said pointedly. "I guess I'll need to stop touching you until you can find the error."

She bit her lip and looked back at the screen. He had threatened to stop touching her but now both of his hands were under her skirt and kneading her bare ass.

She made a sharp gasp when his finger slipped between her cheeks and probed at her anus.

"Stop that." She glared at him.

"Have you ever been fucked in the ass, Ms. Reid?" He asked, his finger pushing once more.

"That's none of your business."

"I'll take that as a no. I think you'd like it. I'd like to show you how good it can feel," he said.

"No thank you," she said so primly that he burst out laughing.

She scanned the screen again. "Tell me it isn't that misspelled 'the'."

"Indeed, it is. Bravo, Ms. Reid."

She glared at him. "You and Jerry called me into a meeting for a single misspelled word? Are you kidding me?"

He shrugged. "Jerry was quite concerned. He said in the two years you've worked here, you've never sent an article for uploading that had a typo in it."

"Maybe it was because I was distracted by you," she said.

"Like I said, a good copy editor can work well even with distractions."

She clenched her hands into fists. God, he drove her crazy. One minute she was hoping he'd put his hand between her legs, and the next minute she wanted to punch him between *his* legs.

"This is ridiculous." She pushed his hands out from under her skirt. "Good night, Mr. Young."

Before she could leave, he stood and pinned her against his desk. She could feel his erection pressing against her ass as he grabbed her wrists and held them tightly.

"We're not quite done yet, Ms. Reid," he whispered into her ear before sucking on the lobe.

She shivered against him as he said, "There is the matter of your discipline."

She twisted her head to look at him. "Are you kidding me? You're going to put a note in my employee file over a misspelled word?"

He grinned. "Of course not. That's just silly. But your error can't go unpunished." He stared at her mouth. "I think a spanking will do. Don't you?"

All of the muscles in Lucy's pelvis tightened in a huge spasm of pleasure, and wetness flooded the crotch of her panties. For one moment she thought she had come just standing there.

How did he know? How did he realize that she fantasized about being spanked? That she wondered what it would feel like to give up that control, and have a hard hand show her how good the mix of pleasure and pain could feel.

Over the years she'd often thought about asking her various boyfriends to spank her. She'd always chickened out, never quite willing to give up the control. Besides, her boyfriends had been shy and a little uncertain in bed. The faceless men in her spanking fantasies always had a confidence about them that allowed her to let go of her inhibitions. The fantasies always ended with her masturbating to a fevered and explosive orgasm.

He cupped her face and sucked on her lower lip. "Have you been spanked before, Ms. Reid?"

She shook her head no and he stared at her for a moment.

"But you want to be." It wasn't a question.

She hesitated and then whispered, "Yes." Her face immediately flamed red with embarrassment.

He rubbed his thumb over her lower lip. "Good, but first..."

His hands reached around her and unbuttoned her suit jacket. He pulled it off of her and dropped it on the floor before grabbing the hem of her camisole and yanking it over her head. He turned her around and lifted her, sitting her on his desk.

"The door." She twisted to look behind her.

"It's locked."

His desk was large and bare except for his phone and laptop. He shoved them both aside and pushed her onto her back. She shivered at the feel of the cold desk on her warm back, and her nipples tightened in the cool air. He leaned over her and pushed her breasts together, licking and sucking and nibbling on her nipples until she was moaning and clutching at his head.

"I've wanted to do that all goddamn week," he muttered against her breast before biting down on her nipple. He tugged on it with his teeth, and she moaned again before he released her nipple and straightened. He pulled her to her feet and turned her around.

"Spread your legs," he demanded.

She parted them and he reached under her jean skirt and hooked his fingers around her panties. He pulled them down and she lifted one boot-clad foot and then the other so he could remove them. He grinned at how wet they were before stuffing them into his pocket.

"You're not keeping those," she said.

He laughed. "I do seem to be getting quite the collection of your panties. Don't I, Ms. Reid?"

Before she could reply he spread her legs farther apart and pushed her down onto his desk. He stretched her arms out, guiding them to the far edge.

"Hold on to the edge," he said.

She curled her fingers around the edge of the desk obediently as he reached for the hem of her skirt and pushed it up until it was bunched around her waist. He ran his hands over her ass and she jerked a little, her hands releasing the edge of the desk.

"Don't let go of the desk," he instructed. She latched on to the desk again as he leaned over her, running his fingers up her bare spine.

"We'll start with five," he said. "Each time you let go of the desk, I'll add another one. Do you understand?"

Lucy nodded. She was stretched out as far as she could go. Just the toes of her boots brushed against the floor, and she could feel the smooth, cold wood of the desk pressing against her breasts, cheek and stomach. With her skirt around her waist and her legs spread, she felt open and vulnerable. Instead of being disturbed by it, she was undeniably turned on.

She expected him to warn her, to maybe ask her if she was ready. So, when the first slap happened it shocked her into letting go of the desk and rising a little. He pushed her back down, his big hand gentle against her back.

"That's another one," he said.

She squeezed the edge of the desk. Her ass was stinging but her nipples were as hard as glass. Her breath was coming in short pants and her pussy was throbbing and pulsing so hard she wasn't sure she could stop herself from coming against his desk.

He spanked her again, his hard hand bouncing off the flesh of her ass and she bit back a moan of pleasure.

"Much better, Ms. Reid," he murmured before rubbing her ass.

He spanked her for a third time. The sound echoed in his office and she wondered briefly if they could hear it in the hallway. Before she could think about it too much, he had spanked her again. This one was the hardest one yet and she jerked against his desk, her hands loosening and her pussy rubbing against the smooth desk.

"I'm starting to wonder if you're letting go of the desk on purpose, Ms. Reid." He leaned over her and licked her spine from just above her ass to between her shoulder blades. She moaned and wiggled, her breath squeezing out of her lungs in harsh gasps.

"Are you?" he whispered in her ear.

"No," she moaned quietly.

He bit her shoulder as he spanked her for a fifth time. She reared up but didn't let go of the desk. Her fingers were white as they clung to the wood, and he kissed her cheek.

"Well done, little Lucy. Only two more to go."

She lifted her head and kissed him, her tongue darting into his mouth. He sucked on it before tearing his mouth from hers.

"Stop distracting me, Ms. Reid," he admonished.

"I wasn't, I -"

She let out a soft squeal as he spanked her hard twice in a row.

She started to rise, and he pushed her back down with a soft thump. "Not yet, pretty Lucy."

She buried her face in her arm, muffling her loud groan when she felt his mouth on her ass. He kissed it repeatedly, soothing the sting of his slaps with his tongue and lips.

He ran his hands up her thighs and spread them a little further. She felt his warm breath briefly on the lips of her pussy before his warm, wet tongue slid between them and licked her hard and swollen clit.

She came immediately, clamping her hand over her mouth at the last moment to muffle her loud scream of pleasure. She shuddered and shook wildly on his desk as he continued to lick her clit. She tried to wiggle away from him, the sensation of his tongue on her swollen clit too much, but he wrapped his hands around her thighs. He held her still, forcing her to feel several more strokes of his tongue before he finally released her.

He leaned over her, his breath warm and ticklish in her ear. "I told you I could make you come with my mouth in less than three minutes."

He traced her spine with his fingers, running them down over her ass and back between her legs. He slid his middle finger into her tight warmth, and she moaned and thrust herself against his hand.

He pulled his hand away and brought his finger up to her mouth, pushing it past her lips. She sucked on it, cleaning her taste from his finger as he watched her hungrily.

"Such a sweet tasting little pussy," he said. "And so very wet. I think you enjoyed your spanking, my pretty Lucy."

He pulled away from her and she was dimly aware of the sound of his zipper and the rustle of a condom wrapper. She slid back a little until her feet were planted on the ground and started to push away from the desk. His hard hand immediately pushed her back onto the desk and held her there until she relaxed.

She looked behind her to see Jason, his t-shirt off and his jeans and underwear around his ankles, rolling a condom onto his deliciously hard cock.

"Jason, wait," she said. "We can't have sex in your office. It's not -"

He stepped between her legs, shoving her feet apart with his and spreading her legs wide. He braced his hard thighs against hers so that she couldn't close her legs.

"Since you've turned down my invitation to come to my house tonight so that I can fuck you in my very large - and very comfortable I might add - bed, I'm just going to have to fuck you right here," he panted.

He grabbed her hips, lifted them, and shoved his hard cock deep into her pussy. She grunted in surprise and braced her hands on the desk as he slammed his cock in and out of her. She moaned low in her throat and shoved her hips back at him.

He groaned loudly. Lucy squeezed her muscles around his cock, and he jerked against her.

"Stop that," he said.

"Something wrong, Mr. Young?" She grinned cheekily at him over her shoulder.

He growled and slapped her hard on the ass. She yelped softly and he let his breath out in a long hiss when she involuntarily squeezed his cock again.

"If you try to make me come before I want to, I will put you over my knee and spank you again after I'm done fucking you. Do you understand?" he said.

She shivered with pleasure and gasped out a breathless yes.

He clenched his jaw and fucked her with long, slow strokes as she moaned and wriggled beneath him. He grabbed hold of the end of her ponytail in his hand, tugging on it until her head came back. He gripped her hair and nuzzled her ear.

"I have never fucked a pussy as wet and tight as yours," he whispered hoarsely into her ear. "You fit me like a glove."

He cupped one breast and tugged on her hair. "Do you like being fucked against my desk, pretty little Lucy?"

She didn't reply and he pulled her hair again. "Do you?"

"Yes," she moaned. "Your cock feels so good, Jason."

He sped up, his cock sliding noisily in and out of her soaking wet pussy, and she shook under him as she reached for her second orgasm.

"Come to my house tonight, Lucy," he said. "Please."

She opened her mouth to moan out a yes when his phone intercom suddenly buzzed. She froze as Carol's voice filled the room.

"Mr. Young? Your four o'clock is here."

"Thank you. Can you take him to the boardroom? I'm just finishing up my meeting with Ms. Reid."

Lucy couldn't believe how normal he sounded. He didn't even sound winded as Carol replied and disconnected the call.

As soon as he heard the click of the intercom, Jason started fucking her hard and fast. He held her hips and plunged in and out of her. Lucy flattened her upper body to the desk and lifted her ass up, giving him even deeper access to her wet pussy. He groaned and reached between their bodies. He dampened his thumb with her juices until it was slick and dripping.

Lucy's orgasm was only a clit stroke away. Her pussy tightened around Jason's hard cock and her legs shook wildly. Jason's hand pressed between her shoulder blades, pinning her down before his thumb slid deep into her ass with sudden, shocking intimacy. She arched her back and buried her mouth in her arm as the most powerful orgasm of her life engulfed her body. His hard cock in her pussy and the firm, unexpected pressure of his thumb in her ass made her convulse helplessly with pleasure.

With a low cry, Jason moved both of his hands back to her hips. He held her tightly as he thrust in and out before coming violently inside of her. She crumpled onto his desk. He collapsed on top of her, she could feel his heartbeat pounding against her back, before kissing her bare shoulder. He pulled out of her, disposed of the condom and pulled his jeans and shirt back on as she straightened and tugged down her skirt. He helped her into her camisole and jacket, cupping her breasts again and kissing her on the mouth, before she buttoned her jacket.

She smiled shakily. "How does my hair look?"

He grinned. "It looks good."

She held her hand out. "Give me back my panties."

He walked to the door of his office and she followed him unsteadily. Her legs were weak and trembling, and little beats of pleasure were still pulsing through her body. "Jason, give me my underwear."

He watched with amusement as she walked toward him. "Are you okay, little Lucy? You seem to be having trouble walking."

"I'm fine," she grumbled. She tried to reach into his pocket and snag her underwear.

He pushed her up against his door, pinned her arms above her head, and kissed her hard on the mouth. "Come by my house tonight and I'll give both pairs back to you."

"Jason, I -"

He pulled her away from the door and opened it.

"Thanks very much, Ms. Reid," he said. "Have a nice weekend."

She glared at him as she followed him down the hallway. He had his hands stuffed in his pockets and he was whistling softly under his breath. If her legs weren't trembling so badly, she would have caught up to him and smacked the smug look from his face.

They parted ways at the bathrooms. As he pushed open the door to the men's room, he pulled a bit of her panties out of his pocket and showed it to her.

She scowled at him and hurried into the ladies' room. She gripped the sink and stared at herself in the mirror. Once again, her mouth was swollen and red but at least her hair wasn't sticking out everywhere. She had just let her boss spank her, fuck her, and put his thumb in her ass. Not to mention the fact that he had stolen a second pair of her underwear. And she had loved every goddamn minute of it. She had obviously gone completely insane.

She had just returned to her desk when her new cell phone buzzed in her purse. It was from Jason. He had texted her the address of his house with a simple, 'See you at seven.'

She shivered and shut down her email. She was going to go home, have a strong drink and a long shower, and decide whether or not she would go to Jason's house and tumble into complete madness.

# CHAPTER 5

Lucy stepped out of her car and smoothed her dress down. She was wearing a dark blue empire-style dress that cupped her breasts like a second skin and showed a generous amount of cleavage. She had paired it with strappy, high-heeled sandals. It was perhaps a bit too summery for early September. Although the days were still warm and sunny, it tended to cool off at night and she probably should have at least brought a thin sweater with her.

It was too late now. She was standing in front of Jason's house and her stomach was a sudsy stew of nerves and desire. She'd been surprised when she pulled up to his house. She expected a large and pretentious house and instead, discovered a small cottage with a tiny front porch. She had to double check the address that Jason had texted her, certain that she was at the wrong house.

She took a deep breath, filling her lungs with the good clean smell of the ocean, and started up the cobblestone pathway. She climbed the steps of the porch and stood in front of the door. The front of the cottage was painted a warm cream colour, but the door was painted a bright and cheery red.

She raised her hand to knock and then hesitated. It wasn't too late. She could still get back in her car and drive home to her quiet, safe apartment. But, if she was honest with herself, she didn't really want to play it safe. There was something about Jason. Something about the way he took control, the way he touched her and brought her so easily to body-shuddering orgasm, that had her craving him in a way she had never craved a man before. Everything about him turned her on, and she couldn't deny that she wanted to experience all that his hard body and sweet words promised. Still, she was playing a dangerous game - one that could cost her job. Her common sense, which was left in the dust for the last few hours, suddenly roared back to life and she took a step backward. Before she could turn and run, the door opened, and Jason stood in the doorway.

He wore a white t-shirt and a pair of shorts and she suddenly felt incredibly overdressed. His feet were bare, and she watched as he used one of them to push the large black cat that was weaving around his feet, back into the cottage.

"Lucy!" He grinned in delight and ushered her into the house. As she stepped into the cool interior and waited for her eyes to adjust to the dim light, Jason looked her up and down. She wondered what he was thinking. Unlike her work attire that concealed and downplayed her breasts, her dress showcased her chest.

"Jason? Why do you look like that?"

"I'm trying very hard not to just pick you up and carry you to my bedroom like a caveman," he said.

She blushed and slipped her shoes off, feeling nervous and uncertain about her decision to join him. He leaned forward and kissed her on the cheek.

"You look beautiful, Lucy."

"Thank you." She hesitated. "I think I might be a bit over-dressed."

He grinned at her. "Trust me, sweetheart. You could have shown up on my doorstep in nothing but a towel and I'd think you were overdressed."

He laughed when she blushed again and then took her hand, leading her into the kitchen. She glanced around curiously. Although the cottage was obviously older, the kitchen was brand new. Stainless steel appliances, granite countertops and sleek, grey cupboards gave it a modern look and feel.

"I like your place," she said.

"Thanks. It's small but since it's just me and Lenny, I figured we didn't need a big place." He walked to one of the cupboards and pulled out two wine glasses.

"Lenny?"

He pointed to the cat that was sitting a few feet away from her and staring unblinkingly at her.

"Ahh." She crouched down and rubbed her fingers together. "Here kitty, kitty."

Lenny stood and walked over. She rubbed the side of his face and smiled a little when he purred and butted his head against her knee.

"He's cute. Where did you get him?"

Jason opened a bottle of wine, the muscles in his arms bulging as he pulled the cork from the bottle with a soft popping noise.

He poured wine into the glasses. "He showed up on my doorstep one day. He was skinny and dirty and covered in fleas. I fed him some tuna and the next thing I knew he was making his dirty, flea-covered self comfortable on my couch. I took him to the vet, got him neutered and cleaned up, and brought him back home. That was a couple of years ago."

"That was nice of you."

He shrugged. "I like animals."

She glanced behind her and into the living room. It had a small fireplace on the far wall with a flat-screen TV mounted above it. A bookshelf crammed with books, a brown leather couch and matching leather chair nearly filled the tiny room.

She jumped a little when his warm voice murmured in her ear. "Would you like a tour of the place? I can show you the den and the bedroom if you'd like."

She shivered at the mention of his bedroom and darted a quick look out the French doors that were off the kitchen. "The sun is starting to set."

He followed her gaze. "So it is, and I did promise you a sunset." He swept her hair over the front of her shoulder and dropped a warm kiss on the back of her neck. "A tour once it's dark then."

She shivered again as he picked up the wine glasses. He handed one to her and then put his hand in the small of her back and led her outside to the back deck. Just the feel of his hand on her back was sending tingles along her spine, and she took a deep breath and tried to calm her pounding heart.

The smell of the ocean filled her nostrils and she stared delightedly in front of her. The deck faced the long, golden beach, and she watched as the waves crashed against the shore. The sun hung low on the horizon and sent beams of light across the water where they flashed like fire.

"It's so beautiful."

"I knew you would like it." He led her to the long futon that was crammed onto the small deck.

She sat down, sipping at her wine and shifting nervously when he sat down next to her. His hip and shoulder brushed against hers, and he took his own sip of wine before putting his arm around her. He rubbed her shoulder and stared out at the ocean.

"I'm really glad you decided to come over tonight, Lucy."

She smiled tentatively at him and he slipped his hand under her hair and cupped her neck. He pulled her toward him and kissed her. His mouth was warm with the rich taste of wine, and she moaned softly and let him slide his tongue between her lips.

They kissed hungrily for a few moments until he pulled back and smiled at her. Lucy didn't object when he took the glass of wine from her hand and set it down next to his on the small table that was beside the futon.

He continued to kiss her, shifting closer and draping her legs over his lap. His fingers kneaded at the back of her neck, and he used his other hand to trace small circles on her collarbone.

She threaded her fingers through his dark hair, cupping his head and pulling him closer as he cupped her breast. He rubbed her nipple through her dress and bra as he kissed his way down her neck. He licked her soft skin and inhaled.

"You always smell so good, Lucy," he whispered.

"You smell good too." She sat back and gave him another nervous smile before looking out over the deck at the setting sun.

"I'm jealous that you get to see this every night."

He sighed with barely hidden disappointment and handed her wine glass back to her. She took it with a small nod of thanks but when she tried to swing her legs off his lap he tightened his grip around her lower legs.

"I love living by the ocean." He took a sip of wine. "Being able to grab my board and walk thirty feet to the waves has always been a dream of mine."

"You surf?"

He nodded. "Does that surprise you?"

"A little," she admitted. "You don't look like the typical surfer."

"What does a typical surfer look like?" he teased.

"Not you." She took another drink of wine and tried to suppress the shudder of need that went through her when he slipped his hand under her dress and stroked one thigh.

"I'm really glad you came over, Lucy," he repeated. "I wasn't sure if you would or not."

"I wasn't sure I would either. What we're doing is -"

She paused and he grinned at her. "A hell of a lot of fun?"

"Yes, but also inappropriate."

"Ahh yes, the inappropriateness of it all." He suddenly turned serious. "While I'll admit that what we did in my office this afternoon definitely falls outside the boundaries of appropriate office behaviour, which I'm entirely blaming you for by the way, there isn't -"

"Me?" She stared at him in shock. "How was that my fault?"

"Let's see," he began to tick off the points on his fingers, "you came to work braless, you practically begged me to touch your pussy in the filing room -"

She started to protest but he ignored her. "You obviously wanted to suck my cock in your office and if you hadn't so clearly enjoyed the spanking I gave you, I imagine I wouldn't have felt such a pressing need to fuck you right then and there."

She gaped at him, her cheeks so red they felt like they were on fire, and he burst out laughing. "I'm just teasing you, Ms. Reid. I would have fucked you even if your sweet pussy hadn't been dripping all over my desk once I was done spanking you."

"Oh my God," she groaned, and he rubbed her thigh again.

"The point I was trying to make is that I looked into the office policy about coworkers dating."

She looked at him in surprise as he continued. "There were no defined rules about it. There should be but I think because the company started out so small and has grown so quickly in the past few months, Darlene in HR hasn't gotten around to updating policies."

He squeezed her thigh. "So, until she gets around to updating the policies on inter-office romance, we're in the clear. No one's getting fired."

She frowned. "We're not just coworkers, Jason. You're my boss."

He shrugged. "Technically I'm not. You report to Jerry as your direct supervisor. I might run the company, but I wouldn't be allowed to fire you without Jerry's approval first."

He took her wine glass and deposited it on the table once more before tugging her toward him. "So, you see, sweet little Lucy, there isn't any reason we can't continue to bring each other so much pleasure."

She hesitated and he stroked her bottom lip with his thumb. "We fit together so well, Lucy. You know we do. I love the way you taste, the way you look, the way you fit so tightly around my cock. I love your submissiveness to me."

"I'm not submissive." She tried to sound firm, but it sounded like a lie, even to her.

"Open your mouth," he demanded. His mouth hovered over hers and her lips parted before she even realized what she was doing.

He kissed her before cupping the back of her head. "Maybe you haven't been submissive with other men but you are with me. You know that, and it's part of the reason why there's this attraction between us."

He shifted her even closer. "Always so calm and cool under pressure, and always keeping yourself under such tight control. It excites you to give up that control in the bedroom, doesn't it? You like the way it feels when I'm the one in control, don't you?"

"Yes." There was no point in denying it.

He kissed the line of her jaw. "There are so many pleasures I can show you, sweet Lucy. You're naturally submissive in bed and I'm naturally dominant. Let me introduce you to things you've only dreamed about."

"I'm not into pain, Jason." She flushed a little. "Spanking is one thing but -"

"I'm not into pain either, Lucy. Nor would I ever do anything to you that you didn't want me to do. I promise you. I would never hurt you."

He kissed her jaw again. "Do you believe me?"

"Yes," she said.

"Good." He turned her head so she was staring out at the water and then nuzzled her neck.

"Are you enjoying the sunset?" He slid his hand further up her dress.

"Yes." She shifted her legs apart to give him better access to her warm core.

His fingers found warm, wet skin where there should have been material and he looked at her in delight. "Why, Ms. Reid. No panties at all?"

"I didn't want a third pair stolen," she replied tartly, and his deep laugh warmed her thoroughly.

He suddenly shifted her and pressed her downward until she was lying on her back on the futon. He started to push her dress up and she tugged it back into place.

"Jason, your neighbours," she protested.

He kissed her bare knee, tracing tiny circles on it with his tongue. "My neighbours to the right are on holidays and the house to the left is empty. There's no one here but you and me, sweet Lucy."

He pushed her hands away. "Keep watching the sunset."

She turned her head obediently and stared at the stunning sight of the sun disappearing below the horizon. The water seemed to dance with light from the setting sun, and she stared mesmerized as Jason pushed her dress up around her hips.

She shivered at the cool air slipping between her thighs when Jason pushed them apart. He kissed the inside of her thighs, trailing his tongue across the sensitive skin as she gasped and looked down at him.

"The sunset, Ms. Reid," he said. "You're going to miss it."

She groaned and dragged her eyes back to the ocean as Jason kissed his way to the juncture of her thighs. At the first feel of his hot breath on her soft curls, she jerked against him, her hips rising up until his mouth brushed against her.

"Naughty girl," he whispered. He pressed her hips back into the soft mattress of the futon. "Stay still."

Lucy was staring at the sunset, but she had no idea what it looked like. Every nerve ending was sizzling and singing as Jason used his fingers to part the wet lips of her pussy. He made a soft noise of approval at the sight of her swollen clit. When he dipped his head and licked it with his warm, flat tongue she was helpless to stop her hips from bucking against him.

"Oh, oh, oh…" she moaned. Her hands, which were clenching the mattress of the futon, moved to grip his head and she shoved him deeper into her. He traced around her clit with the tip of his tongue before he moved his mouth to her wet opening and probed it with his tongue.

She cried out. His stubble against her skin created a tantalizing combination of pleasure and pain, and she rubbed herself against him as he replaced his tongue with two fingers. He licked her clit repeatedly as he thrust his fingers in and out of her before pressing them against the front inside wall of her pussy. That created a brand new sensation, one that had her nearly falling off the futon, and he pressed his left arm across her stomach to anchor her in place. He held her down as he continued to pleasure her with his tongue and fingers.

Her orgasm was building inside of her. His hot mouth and his probing fingers worked together to bring her to a frenzy of need, and she couldn't stop the loud whimpers and moans of pleasure from escaping her lips.

She looked down at Jason's dark head burrowed between her pale thighs at the exact moment he sucked on her clit. The erotic sight of his head between her legs and the pressure of his lips around her swollen, throbbing clit threw her into the abyss. She cried out, her thighs tightening around Jason's head, as lightning bolts of pleasure ran through her pelvis and legs. Shaking and shuddering, she fell back against the futon, panting harshly as Jason raised his head and slid up her body. He covered her body with his and kissed her on the mouth. She could taste herself on his lips and it sent a new pang of arousal through her.

"Should I give you that tour now?" he panted against her mouth.

She could barely catch her own breath, but she nodded and said, "Yes, I think a tour is a very good idea."

# CHAPTER 6

Jason stood and helped her stand up, pushing her dress back down. Her legs were like jelly and he bent and scooped her up, carrying her into the house.

She licked his neck before sucking on his earlobe. He groaned and strode down a small hallway before stopping in front of the first closed door on the left.

"This is the den" he muttered as she nipped at his neck.

"It looks nice," she replied without looking up.

His arms tightened around her when she slid her hand inside his shirt and ran her fingers through the hair on chest. He moved further down the hallway, his breath catching when Lucy scraped her fingernails across one flat nipple.

"Jesus," he groaned and jerked his head towards the next door. "Bathroom."

"Mm-hmm." She kissed his jaw, running her tongue across the stubble and enjoying the slight sting.

He walked to the door at the end of the hallway. "Bedroom."

She moved her hand, searching blindly for the doorknob. Her fingers brushed against it and she turned it as he pushed on the bottom of the door with his foot. He carried her into the room. His bedroom faced the ocean and the light from the dying sun filled the room with a warm, golden glow. It was a small room and completely dominated by the biggest bed Lucy had ever seen.

"Good God." She stared at the bed. "Three people could sleep stretched out on this bed and not touch once."

"I think it's a little early for us to be talking about inviting someone else into the bed with us. Maybe next weekend," he replied.

She blushed and smacked him lightly on the back. "That isn't what I meant, you pervert."

He laughed and set her on her feet next to the bed. "You should perhaps work on your communication skills, Ms. Reid."

He reached for the hem of her dress and she lifted her arms so he could pull it over her head. He removed her bra and stared reverently at her breasts before cupping them in his large hands.

"So beautiful," he murmured. He dipped his head and kissed each nipple before sucking on them.

She arched her back and reached for his shirt. She unbuttoned it and pushed it off his shoulders. He shrugged out of it, letting it fall to the floor, and she reached for the button on his shorts. She unbuttoned them and slipped her hand inside of them, gasping in surprise at his own lack of underwear.

"I was afraid you might try to steal my underwear in retaliation," he said. She had a quick image of stuffing his underwear into her purse and burst into giggles.

"You find my lack of underwear amusing?" He pinched her nipple. She gasped and twisted her hand until she was gripping his hard cock. He made his own gasp and let his head fall back as she stroked him.

"Not at all," she said. She used her other hand to unzip his shorts and they fell to the floor. She looked down, desire unfurling in her belly at the sight of his cock. She ran her thumb over the tip of it, spreading the moisture across it as he gave another groan of pleasure.

She turned him around and pushed him into a sitting position on his bed. She knelt between his legs and bent her head, taking the tip of his cock into her warm mouth. He inhaled sharply and his hands threaded into her hair. He gripped her head and urged her mouth lower. She slid her mouth down, taking as much of his large cock into her mouth as she could. She sucked his cock with long, slow strokes of her mouth as she gripped the base with her hand and twisted lightly.

"Oh my God, Lucy," he muttered as his hips moved with the motion of her mouth.

She pulled her mouth free and pressed against his hips. "Stay still, Mr. Young," she demanded.

She put his hands on the side of the bed, watching with some amusement as his fingers curled into the quilt. He shuddered under her as she took his cock into her mouth again. For long moments there was nothing but the sound of his loud groans as she licked and sucked and stroked him.

"Lucy, stop!" Jason gasped out. He tugged her to her feet as she blinked at him in surprise.

"What's wrong?"

"Nothing," he ground out. "You're going to make me come if you keep doing that."

She grinned and started to bend over him again. He growled and twisted his hand in her hair, pulling on it until she was staring up at him. "If I didn't know better, Ms. Reid, I'd think you were deliberately trying to provoke me into spanking you again."

A spasm of pleasure, so deep it nearly hurt, flooded

through her pelvis and lower belly and she bit down on her lower lip.

He groaned at the look on her face. "Jesus Christ, Lucy. You have no idea what you do to me."

He kissed her hard, nearly shoving his tongue into her mouth. She returned his kiss, standing between his legs and pressing herself against him. His cock brushed against her soft curls and they both gasped. He reached around her and grabbed her ass, pulling him against her and letting his cock press against the curve of her stomach.

He broke the kiss and gently pushed her away. She watched as he scooted back on the bed until his back was resting against the headboard, and his long legs were stretched out in front of him. There was a small bedside table next to the bed, and he opened the single drawer and pulled out a condom. He rolled it on and then held his hand out to her.

"Come here."

She climbed onto the bed. She was a little embarrassed by how quickly Jason had recognized her uncharacteristic desire to submit to him in bed, and she was determined to show him the other side of her. She was used to making men beg her to come, and she knew that riding Jason would allow her to control the pace and have him pleading to come in minutes. She grinned as she straddled him, her thighs planted around his hips and her full breasts nearly brushing his mouth.

"Something funny, Ms. Reid?" He raised one eyebrow at her as he settled his hands onto her hips.

"No." She kissed him on the mouth, already hearing in her head the sound of his sexy voice begging and pleading with her.

She rose up and pushed herself onto his hard cock, taking half of him into her. He cried out with pleasure as she waited for her slick core to stretch around him. She leaned forward and braced her hands on the headboard, pushing her breasts toward his mouth. He suckled hard on one nipple and she arched her back and let her head fall back, her long dark hair tickling his thighs.

She slid up and down his cock, refusing to take more than half of his hardness into her and turning her hips in a spiraling motion as she rode him slowly. His fingers dug into her hips as she moved. She reached between them and rubbed her clit, her fingers pressing and circling in the way she liked best. She wanted to come again - needed to come again - and she moved her fingers faster. She tightened her muscles around his cock as she rose up until just the head of him was planted in her.

She was so close, and the fiery need was growing in her pelvis. She was only vaguely aware of Jason's hands leaving her hips. She cried out with surprise when his hard hands closed around her wrists and yanked her fingers away from her throbbing clit. Before she could stop him, he had pinned her arms behind her back with one strong hand.

He used his other hand to cup the back of her neck and push her down until she was impaled fully on his hard shaft. She yanked at his hand and wiggled her body, trying to free herself as he watched her with some amusement.

"Jason, let me go!" She pouted and twisted some more, trying to use her legs to push herself upward. It was useless. Jason was much stronger than she was and even as her mind rebelled, her pussy grew steadily wetter at being so completely and easily subdued.

"I want to come." She tried to keep the pleading note out of her voice and failed miserably.

"I know you do, sweet Lucy." He dipped his head and

kissed both of her breasts before licking the hollow between them.

She moaned and arched her back when he took one taut nipple between his teeth and pulled on it, stretching it out before releasing it. "But as much as I love watching you touch your pussy, I don't want you to come just yet."

"Let go of my hands," she said. "I promise I won't touch myself."

He grinned. "I don't believe you, little Lucy. I bet the minute I let you go, your fingers will be touching your pussy and you'll be riding me hard enough to make me come."

He moved under her, thrusting his hips back and forth. She moaned as his hard cock rubbed against her soft walls. He moved his hand from her neck and around her back to take a wrist in each hand. He pulled on her arms until she was forced to arch her back and then he thrust harder into her. She cried out and rode him helplessly, her large breasts bouncing and her pussy squeezing his cock as he drove into her repeatedly.

"Do you want to come, Lucy?" he growled.

"Yes, oh yes!" she cried out breathlessly.

"Not yet," he said and slowed his hard thrusts until he was barely moving within her.

She writhed on top of him, yanking at his hands and bouncing her hips against his. Her pussy was so wet she had drenched his cock and the tops of his thighs. She should have been embarrassed by it, but the wet sucking sounds her pussy made as his cock slid in and out of her only heightened her desire.

"Behave or I'll make you suck my cock again before I let you come," he said.

She bit her lip and forced herself to stay still. She was so close to coming. Her entire body throbbed with need. She kissed him hard on the mouth, darting her tongue into its warm recesses and brushing her breasts against his chest.

"Please, Jason," she panted into his mouth.

"Please what?" She could tell that Jason's own control was slowly eroding. He gritted his teeth and groaned out loud when her muscles squeezed compulsively around his hard length.

"Please fuck me. Please make me come. Oh please, Jason," she begged.

The sound of her voice and her whimpers of need must have pushed him over the edge. He tightened his grip on her wrists and fucked her hard and fast. She came almost immediately, her pussy squeezing his cock in a vice grip. He shouted hoarsely and came as well, pumping in and out of her a few more times as she collapsed against him.

He released her wrists and she slid from his body like a wet noodle. She curled up on her side as he disposed of the condom and relaxed behind her. He pulled her ass up against his pelvis and put his arm around her waist, cupping her breast as she sighed.

"That was amazing," she said as she brushed her hair from her face.

"I hurt you," Jason said.

"Hmm?"

"Your wrists." He took her left hand in his and rubbed his thumb across the red welts on her wrists.

"They don't hurt."

"I held you too tightly," he fretted.

"No, you didn't. I," she hesitated, "I liked it."

He kissed her bare shoulder. "I liked it too. Next time we'll use a scarf, just as effective and won't leave such red marks." He brought her hand back and kissed her wrist as a blush rose on her pale skin.

He rolled her onto her back and leaned over her, kissing the tip of her nose and brushing her hair away from her face.

"Will you stay the night with me, little Lucy?"

"Yes, I'd like that."

"Good. Now tell me about the bet."

His sudden change of topic took her so off guard that she almost blurted out the details of the office bet to him.

"I don't know what the bet is," she lied.

He laughed. "You're a horrible liar, Ms. Reid."

He kissed her slowly, his fingers kneading her breast. Despite her recent orgasm, her body responded to his touch.

"Tell me what this bet is that Alex and Maureen were talking about," he coaxed as his hand slipped down her belly and cupped her sex.

"No fair," she complained. "You're distracting me."

He slipped his index finger between the wet lips of her pussy and rubbed at her still-sensitive clit. "Do you know I've never been with a woman who gets as wet as you do?"

She groaned in embarrassment. "Oh my God."

"That's not something to be embarrassed about. Believe me." He pushed his pelvis against her hip. She started a little when she felt his semi-hard cock against her flesh.

"Just thinking about how wet you get makes me hard. In the last five months I've had more erections than I've ever had in my life. Not to mention a serious case of blue balls."

Before she could ask him what he meant by that, he moved his hand back to her waist and squeezed. "Tell me about the bet."

She had hoped he had forgotten about it, but it was obvious he wasn't going to let it go. "It's just a stupid office bet that Alex started."

"Go on," he prompted.

"The ladies in the office started a bet a few months ago

about who could bed you first. There's even a prize for it – a weekend at the 'Heaven's Gate Spa'."

He didn't say anything, and she glanced up at him. "Are you angry?"

He laughed. "No. Just surprised."

She rolled her eyes. "That the women in the office want to sleep with you? Pul-lease. You know exactly how sexy you are, Mr. Young."

He actually blushed a little and she grinned delightedly as he looked down at her. "You said there was a prize?"

She nodded. "Yeah, spa getaway."

"But this morning in the filing room Alex said she was determined to win the bet. I'm pretty sure you won that bet last Friday. I mean, I guess technically it wasn't a bed we were in but still..."

"I wasn't invited to join the bet, and even if I were, I wouldn't have told them anyway. My personal life is private," she said.

"Why weren't you invited to join the bet?"

"Well, because of the way I look and because you were always so cold and borderline rude to me. Also, I wasn't fawning over you like the rest of the women in our office. Alex and the others assumed you hated me. Hell, until that day in the elevator I thought you hated me."

He sighed. "I'm sorry, Lucy. I was distant and rude because I was trying to hide how much I wanted you. I've been attracted to you for months. I could barely stand next to you without getting a goddamn erection. I decided it would be better if I was rude."

She grinned a little. "You did a great job. There's a second bet going around the office on how long it'll take for you to fire me."

He threaded his fingers through her long hair, holding a

piece of it and rubbing it between his fingers. "Shit. I'm sorry."

She shrugged. "It didn't bother me. Well, maybe a little but only because I was fighting my own attraction to you."

"What did you mean when you said you weren't invited to join the bet because of the way you look?"

She gave him a dry look. "Jason, please. You're smart, gorgeous, and have a body like a Greek God. Everyone assumed you liked the model type - Alex's type - and you'd never go for chubby, pale Lucy."

He stared angrily at her. "That's ridiculous. You're sexy and beautiful, and unlike Alex, you can actually carry on an intelligent conversation. I'm lucky to have you in my bed."

He palmed her breast, squeezing it gently. "And I like your curves."

"You're preaching to the choir, baby." She grinned and poked him. "I'm like, ridiculously awesome in every way."

He laughed as she ran her hand across his broad chest. "Also, I'm glad you like the curves because I like them too and they're not going anywhere."

He caught her hand in his and linked their fingers together before staring solemnly at her. "I do like you, Lucy. I'm hoping that this can become more than just about us having sex all the time. I promise to keep our work life and our personal life separate."

She arched her eyebrow at him. "So, you don't want to have sex with me anymore? You just want to talk about our feelings?"

"No!" he nearly shouted. "I definitely want to keep having sex with you. I just thought that maybe we could, I don't know, go to a movie or have dinner and get to know each other a little better."

"Why, Mr. Young. Are you asking me out on a date? Do you think that's appropriate?"

He flushed a little. "I know the work thing is an issue but like I said earlier, I'm not your direct supervisor and -"

She put her hand over his mouth. "Jason, I'm teasing you. I'd love to go on a date with you."

He nipped at her fingers. "I had no idea you were such a tease, Ms. Reid."

"A girl has to have some secrets." She squeaked in alarm when he suddenly straddled her and kissed her neck with warm, wet kisses.

"I'm looking forward to learning all of your secrets," he whispered as his hands moved to cup and knead her breasts.

"I'll let you know one right now," she said breathlessly.

He licked the tip of her nipple until it tightened into a hard bud. "Go ahead."

"I'll be expecting you to put out after our first date." Her fingers pressed into his hard biceps as he laughed and lifted his head to kiss her full mouth.

"Only if you buy me dinner first, Ms. Reid." He kissed her neck again and she shivered at the feel of his rough stubble.

"You have yourself a deal, Mr. Young," she murmured as he covered her body with his.

---

Monday morning Lucy eased her sore body into her office chair. She had spent the entire weekend with Jason, and muscles were hurting that she didn't even know she had.

A plain white envelope with her name written on it was propped on her keyboard. She ripped it open, turning it upside down and shaking the contents out. Her eyes widened at the gift certificate to the 'Heaven's Gate Spa'. There was a folded piece of paper with it and she unfolded it, scanning the words written in Jason's neat writing.

*Ms. Reid,*

*Please accept my invitation to the Heaven's Gate Spa for a couple's massage this weekend. I thought it would be a fitting first date, considering you're the official winner of the office bet.*

*Jason*

Lucy burst into laughter as she tucked the gift certificate and note into her purse. Dating Jason Young would be an adventure and a half.

Keep reading for an excerpt of "Twice Tempted", Book Two in the Tempted Series.

Lucy put her arms around Jason's shoulders and gave him a brief hug. He stood stiffly against her and feeling like a complete moron she stepped back. His hands clenched into fists, and then he wrapped his arms around her waist and pulled her into his embrace. She hugged him and rubbed his back as he buried his face in the curve of her neck.

"I'm so sorry," she repeated.

"Thank you." His reply was muffled against her throat. He lifted his head and stared down at her.

"I just got back into town late this afternoon. I wasn't going to come tonight but I wanted to see you." He stroked her cheek with his thumb. "I missed you."

"I missed you too," she admitted.

"Yeah?"

She smiled a little. "Yeah."

He dipped his head and kissed her. It was just a gentle brush of his mouth against hers, but she immediately flattened her body against him and returned his kiss. His tongue slipped into her mouth and she stroked it with her own as he moaned low in his throat.

He backed her up against the linen closet door and she hooked one leg around his waist, pulling him into her. He unbuttoned her shirt as they kissed hungrily, and then worked his fingers under the cups of her bra and cupped her breasts with his warm hands. He kissed down her throat and she lifted her head to give him better access.

"You're so beautiful, Lucy," he muttered against her collarbone. He nipped it, making her gasp, before running his thumbs over her nipples.

She slipped her hands under his t-shirt and ran them across his bare back, kneading and rubbing at the hard muscles.

"Take off your shirt," she whispered.

He pulled his t-shirt over his head and dropped it onto the counter. She stared appreciatively at his bare chest. Two weeks of being away from the beach had made his skin a little paler but compared to her he still had a rich glow. She ran her fingers through the hair on his chest, and he inhaled sharply when she traced his abs with her short nails.

She slipped her hand into his jeans, pushing past his boxer briefs with impatience until she could wrap her long fingers around his thick cock. He moaned when she gripped him and moved her hand up and down the shaft.

"Shh." She grinned at him.

He slanted his mouth over hers, thrusting his tongue into her mouth as he gripped her thigh in his hand and moved it higher. He squeezed her breast and then ran his hand over the soft swell of her belly under her shirt before his fingers trailed along the inside of her thigh. She thrust her pelvis against him when he traced the material of her underwear.

She stroked his cock faster in response, and he uttered a low curse of need before sliding his fingers under her panties. His thick fingers found her wet opening almost immediately, and he pushed two of them into her. She rocked her hips against him and squeezed his cock.

"That feels so good, little Lucy," he whispered into her ear. "If you keep doing that, I won't be able to stop myself from fucking you right here."

"I don't want you to stop," she whispered.

She stroked him rapidly, feeling the moisture at the tip of him as he moved his fingers in and out of her. She didn't hear a knock and apparently neither did Jason because when the bathroom door opened and Heather stuck her head in, they both froze like frightened rabbits.

"Lucy, are you..." Heather stared at their entwined bodies, her mouth dropping open and her cheeks going pink. "Oh my goodness. Oh – oh my – I'm so, so sorry."

She swung the door shut and Lucy stared wide-eyed at Jason. "Oh shit."

## ABOUT THE AUTHOR

Elizabeth Kelly was born and raised in Ontario, Canada. She moved west as a teenager and now lives in Alberta with her husband and a menagerie of pets. She firmly believes that a person can survive solely on sushi and coffee, and only her husband's mad cooking skills prevents her from proving that theory.

For more information about Elizabeth, check out her website at

www.elizabethkelly.ca

 facebook.com/EKellyBooks

twitter.com/ElizabethKBooks

instagram.com/elizabethkelly_author

amazon.com/Elizabeth-Kelly/e/B00EOHZ0MS

bookbub.com/authors/elizabeth-kelly

ALSO BY ELIZABETH KELLY

**Tempted Series**

Tempted

Twice Tempted

Forever Tempted

Breathless

Tempted Trilogy (Books 1-3)

**Red Moon Series**

Red Moon

Red Moon Rising

Dark Moon

Alpha Moon

Pale Moon

**The Recruit Series**

The Recruit (Book One)

The Recruit (Book Two)

The Recruit (Book Three)

The Recruit (Book Four)

The Recruit (Book Five)

**The Shifters Series**

Willow and the Wolf (Book One)

Ava and the Bear (Book Two)

Katarina and the Bird (Book Three)

Porter's Mate (Book Four)

Bria and the Tiger (Book Five)

Rosalie Undone (Book Six)

The Dragon's Mate (Book Seven)

Rise of the Jaguar (Book Eight)

**The Draax Series**

Reign (Book One)

Rule (Book Two)

Rebel (Book Three)

**Harmony Falls Series**

Sweet Harmony (Book One)

Perfect Harmony (Book Two)

Forbidden Harmony (Book Three)

Redeeming Harmony (Book Four)

**Individual Books**

The Necessary Engagement

Amelia's Touch

The Rancher's Daughter

Healing Gabriel

The Contract

A Home for Lily

Saving Charlotte

Shameless

The Fairy Tales Collection

Broken

An Unlikely Seduction

**Holiday Romance**

The Christmas Wife

The Christmas Rescue

The Christmas Nanny

The Christmas Boss

Sordid Games